EPIC ESCAPE ROOMS

MAXIMISING STUDENT ENGAGEMENT THROUGH THE POWER OF PERSONALISED ESCAPE ROOMS.

Contents

Introduction: (My Story)

<u>A little about me:</u>

I have had the pleasure of teaching the greatest subject (History) for 13 years at Casula High School in Sydney's South-West, NSW, Australia.

The reason why this is arguably the best subject to teach is because there is so much scope to bring the content to life and have so much fun with it.

My primary focus in the classroom is to develop high energy, engaging T & L strategies that result in a passion for learning History.

<u>My context:</u>

Casula High is a co-educational comprehensive high school located in Sydney's South-West. Most classes in our school consist of a vast range of ability levels. We have a high proportion of students who are from an EAL/D (English as an Additional Language or Dialect) background.

<u>Engaging Teaching & Learning:</u>

I realised early in my career, that if I could not make my lessons relevant, engaging and purposeful, I would not be able to sustain the attention of the majority of my students for very long.

After many years of trying various strategies to effectively and sustainably engage a mixed ability classroom, I have become passionate about Escape Rooms, Quiz Shows, Movie-Making, Board Game Design, Walls That Teach, Project-Based Learning and Festival days.

Obviously, it is not sustainable to be able to incorporate high energy tasks into every single lesson, however, it is entirely possible to enhance learning experiences by offering a few of these opportunities throughout the year.

<u>Motivation through Collaboration:</u>

I have discovered extra motivation by sharing my experiences with the History teaching community. Many of my ideas have been inspired by this same community so I have decided to 'pay it forward' whenever I develop a resource that could provide value or inspiration to others. I encourage all teachers to utilise the amazing teaching networks available online. It is a perfect way of connecting with like-minded professionals and building productive networks. Ultimately it is students that benefit from this collective teacher efficacy.

<u>Getting Started:</u>

<u>"Experience is the teacher of all things" – Gaius Julius Caesar:</u>

The first experience I had with 'Escape Rooms' in the classroom was with a disengaged year 9 History class that I was trying to teach WW1 to in 2018. The idea came to me when I recently attempted a commercial Escape Room for the first time outside of school and absolutely fell in love with the concept. I immediately saw lots of potential with incorporating it into the class, but I was very unsure of how I would go about designing one.

Luckily for me, there was a Maths teacher at my school who had been using 'breakouts' in her classroom, so I decided I'd reach out to her for some advice. At the time, our school was promoting cross-KLA partnerships and innovative classroom practice. We decided to go to our Principal and request a 'Professional Learning' day, so that we could work together, focus on our concept and refine the idea. In exchange, we offered to share our experience with staff members at a meeting in the future.

It took a term of intricate planning, but we managed to eventually pull it off and test it out on staff teams and my year 9 class. It did not go smoothly at all. I split the class into two big groups and had half the class outside being supervised with some assigned work while the other half were doing the Escape Room inside. Luckily enough I was able to see through the limitations that had presented itself and see massive potential with this style of task. The one thing that was present even at this early stage was an increase in engagement levels, even from some of my more challenging students.

<u>Reflecting and Refining:</u>

Upon reflection, it was hard to justify spending a term of planning for a 20-minute experience for students, so it took a while to give it another shot in the future.

There are also two notable things that happened which kept this teaching strategy at the forefront of my mind. The first thing was that I had students from other classes who were approaching me and inquiring about the WW1 Escape Room Challenge and asking if they could attempt it after school. The second thing is that I shared some photos with the 'NSW History Teachers' Facebook group and the post exploded with teachers requesting that the resources be sent to them. These two things really helped to reinforce the potential of Escape Rooms in a high-school context.

After years of persevering, reflecting and refining the use of Escape Rooms in my programs, I have acquired numerous tips and tricks to developing effective, engaging, educational, personalised Escape Rooms. The best thing, is that once you have tried it out a few times, you can significantly reduce the amount of time it takes to get one up and running. I have now developed an Escape Room for every single junior and senior topic that I teach and instead of it taking a term of planning, I can usually go from brainstorming to implementation in a few days. It is also my sincere hope that I can assist educators through this book by offering them my experienced advice which will undoubtedly help the beginning stage of the journey.

<u>What you can expect:</u>

I have extracted the most practical aspects of educational Escape Room design and included them throughout the rest of the book. You can expect to receive useful advice which will make you want to start planning your very own educational Escape Rooms.

Before engaging in the planning process, it is crucial to consider Simon Sinek's "Start With Why" notion. This will help you maintain focus throughout the entirety of your Escape Room implementation, just remember your purpose.

Once this is firmly at the forefront of your mind, you will have set yourself up for success throughout the implementation process. I will then guide you through the best tips and tricks that I have accumulated over a lengthy engagement with this innovative teaching & learning strategy, hopefully offering you the best possible insight.

Part 1 – Why?

Integrating Escape Rooms into high school education can offer a range of benefits, fostering both academic and personal development. Students develop and demonstrate a range of skills throughout the process of these lessons. Below are some examples of the benefits of using Escape Rooms in high schools:

<u>Benefits for Students</u>

<u>Team Building and Collaboration:</u>

Communication Skills: Escape Rooms encourage students to communicate effectively with their peers. They must share ideas, listen to others, and work together to solve puzzles. I have witnessed first-hand, some of the most introverted students come out of their shell and excel in these lessons.

Teamwork: Students learn the importance of teamwork and how combining their individual strengths can lead to collective success. This is always a point that is emphasized and obvious when reflecting at the end of the task.

<u>Critical Thinking and Problem-Solving:</u>

Analytical Skills: Escape Rooms present complex puzzles that require critical thinking and analytical reasoning. Students must assess the situation, identify patterns, and devise creative solutions.

Problem-Solving: Students develop problem-solving skills as they work through challenges, fostering resilience and adaptability.

<u>Time Management:</u>

Time Pressure: Escape Rooms often have time constraints, teaching students to manage their time efficiently. The best Escape Rooms will tie their time constraint into the theme. EG – In my Ancient China Escape Room, my students have 60 minutes to find the secret passageway to escape or they will be trapped in the Emperor's tomb for eternity. This skill is valuable in academic settings and future professional endeavours.

<u>Subject Integration:</u>

Escape Room design allows you to incorporate numerous challenges which relate specifically to the content you have taught. An immersive experience will allow students to engage with content areas in a new and exciting way. A wider range of content-based challenges can cater for a more diverse range of learners in your classroom.

<u>Cross-Curricular Learning:</u>

Escape Rooms can be designed to incorporate various subjects, reinforcing academic concepts in a fun and interactive way. For example, math, science, history, or language arts can be integrated into the puzzles.

<u>Intrinsic Motivation:</u>

The engaging and immersive nature of Escape Rooms can motivate students intrinsically. This motivation can positively impact their attitude toward learning.

Active Learning: Escape Rooms provide a hands-on, active learning experience, which can enhance retention and understanding of the material.

<u>Creativity and Innovation:</u>

Design and Implementation: Creating Escape Rooms or even just solving them requires a level of creativity. Students can unleash their imagination when designing puzzles or thinking outside the box to solve challenges. Once you become more advanced with Escape Rooms you will discover that there is potential to include students in the design phases of your rooms. EG – I have had small groups of Escape Room enthusiasts work with me during their spare time to create Escape challenges for other classes.

<u>Stress Management:</u>

Positive Stress: While there is a time constraint, Escape Rooms provide a positive stress environment. Students can learn to manage stress and pressure constructively, which is a valuable life skill.

At the end of each challenge, the class and I debrief about the experience and this is an excellent opportunity to reinforce the skills they have developed.

<u>Interpersonal Skills:</u>

Escape Rooms promote social interaction, helping students develop interpersonal skills. This is particularly beneficial for students who may be shy or introverted. Students begin to realise the importance of clear communication amongst peers. One thing that is often discussed during a debrief session with a class is how the more effective groups worked cooperatively together and respected and utilised all peers throughout the challenges.

<u>Fun Learning Experience:</u>

As Dave Burgess emphasizes in his 'Teach Like a Pirate' mantra "It's ok to have fun in the classroom".[1] To Utilise Seth Goldin's 'Purple Cow' analogy[2], immersive Escape Rooms have the ability to transform lessons into a 'purple cow' for students. A 'purple cow' is something that is remarkable, unbelievable and that stands out from the rest. It is something you will never forget. This style of lesson will stand out to students. They are unlike the majority of teaching and learning strategies that they are exposed to on a day-to-day basis and thus will have a more substantial impact on their education.

<u>Engagement:</u>

Escape Rooms make learning enjoyable and memorable. Students may become more enthusiastic about education when it involves interactive and entertaining activities.

Integrating Escape Rooms into high school education provides a dynamic and innovative approach to learning, addressing various aspects of personal and academic education.

Students learn best when they are engaged! Escape Rooms provide an opportunity for students to play active roles in their classrooms.

---

[1] Burgess, D. (2012). Teach like a pirate : Increase student engagement, boost your creativity, and transform your life as an educator. San Diego, California: Dave Burgess Consulting, Inc.
[2] Godin, S 2009, Purple cow : transform your business by being remarkable, Portfolio, New York.

<u>Develop a love of learning:</u>

Constructive challenges build engaged and capable learners. Escape Rooms allow educators to create a learner-centred experience that allows students to work together, think conceptually, and utilize prior knowledge for deeper comprehension. These experiences possess the key to unlocking a love of learning.

An Escape Room experience doesn't end when players complete the challenge. Learning continues as students reflect on the experience, making new connections as they consider their experience and ask important questions: What went well? What would you do differently next time? Who from your team deserves a shout-out?

<u>Inclusivity:</u>

Students of all academic abilities can participate in an Escape Room experience. Each student can bring a new perspective or a skill set to help the greater good of the team. Whether it is quick mental math, an affinity for puzzles, or leadership skills, players can show off their strengths and feel good about their contributions. Success in an Escape Room experience truly does rely on everyone bringing their own talents and skills and working together.

Benefits for Educators

It is not only the students that will reap the benefits of immersive Escape Rooms. The development of them has a substantial impact on educators also. Some of these benefits include:

<u>Assessment of Individual and Group Performance:</u>

Observation and Evaluation: Teachers can observe and assess students' individual and group performance during Escape Room activities, gaining insights into their strengths and areas for improvement.

Furthermore, it allows the educator the opportunity to observe a vast array of skills which are demonstrated from all students. A perfect way of building a deeper professional relationship.

<u>Reinvigoration:</u>

This may not happen straight away, but I have found that I have developed a new motivated approach when it comes to designing these learning experiences. I am excited to develop, promote, carry out and refine these learning experiences because they are so beneficial to my classes. Monotony in our profession can leave us feeling flat and unmotivated. It is so crucial that we actively seek ways to revitalise our passion for education.

<u>Collaboration:</u>

There are numerous collaboration opportunities when it comes to developing Escape Rooms. I have collaborated with staff within my faculty, in other KLA's and in other schools across the country. The staff members I have collaborated with range from novice to expert in relation to their Escape Room design experience. Regardless of who you work with, the collaboration is always mutually beneficial. It helps spark new ideas, refine existing ones and build strong partnerships.

<u>Leadership Opportunities:</u>

This style of teaching and learning strategy can be quite daunting for people who have had no experience with them, however, once you become confident with it, there will be numerous opportunities which will present themselves in relation to leadership development. I have been asked to present at faculty meetings, staff meetings and at state and national conferences. This is not something which is mandatory, however, I would encourage challenging yourself in this regard. The benefits are endless.

Part 2 – 15 hot tips for getting the most out of Escape Rooms

These are some of the best tips I have picked up after years of testing and refining when it comes to getting the most out of these rooms.

My personalised Escape Rooms have been designed for group sizes ranging from 8-30, ages 12-18. Many of my classes are mixed-ability groups often with high proportions of EAL/D students and low literacy levels. However, each class is different and requires adjustments to be made when planning and delivering these lessons.

Ultimately the best thing you can do is figure out what works for you and personalise the experience for your context.

<u>#1 – Start small, with an easy to manage class, put them in colour coded groups.</u>

The most successful way I have found to run an Escape Room is to split the class into small groups. Depending on the class, I either allow the students to choose their own groups or I allocate the groups using a random group creator website/app.

The ideal group size is about 4-6 students; however, challenges can be added/altered if group sizes are going to be larger.

These groups are given a colour, team name and team captain. I use coloured dot stickers on all Escape Room challenges so that the groups know which challenges are for them to solve/complete.

A formula that I have which works well is to set up the final lock box as a hasp lock which can be locked with multiple padlocks (see images on the next page). This allows one group to finish their part without the final room being complete.

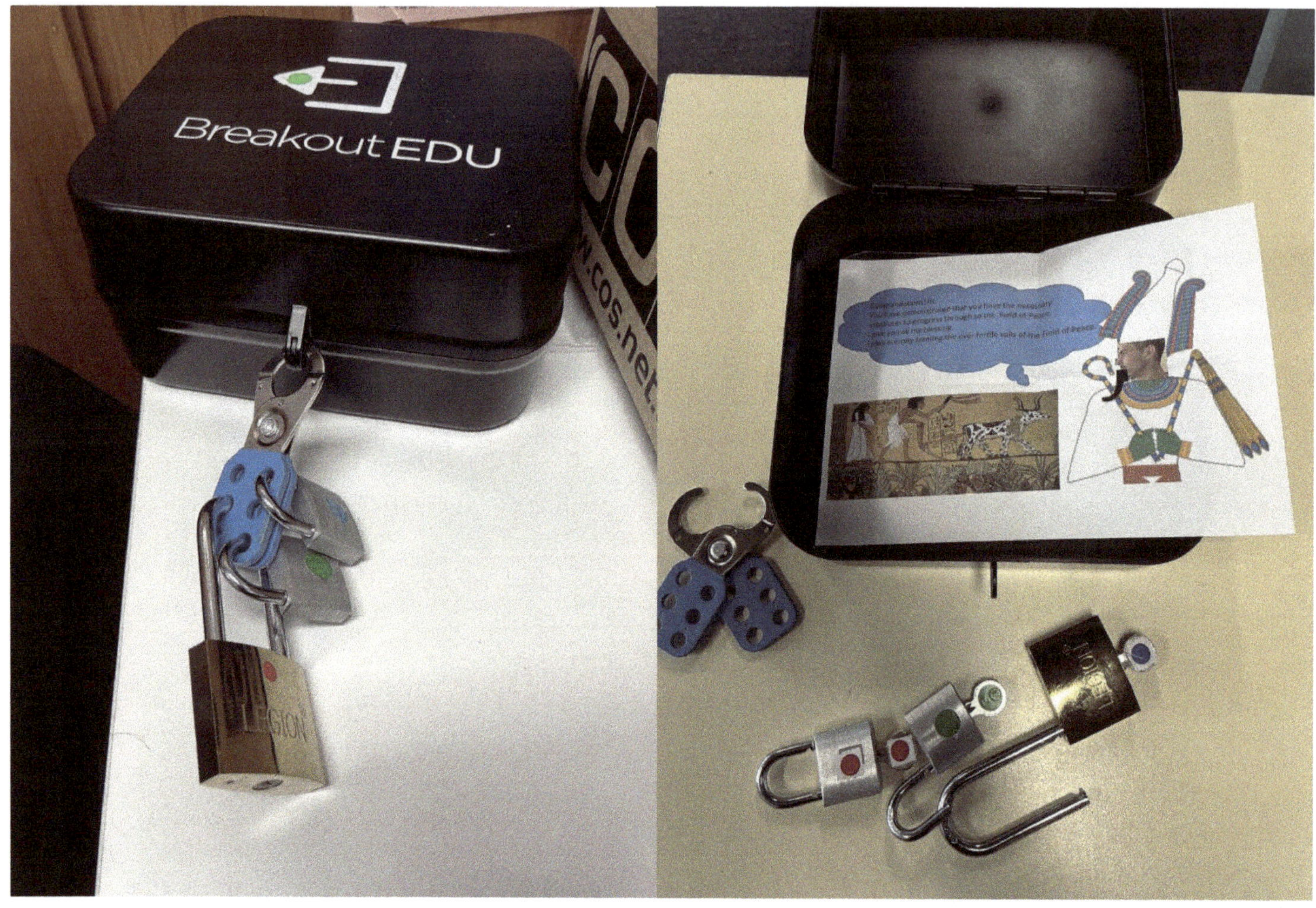

Breakout EDU box concealing final task using a hasp lock. All coloured teams must unlock their padlock for the box to reveal its contents.

This is ideal because it simultaneously promotes competition and collaboration. Each group wants to be the first to locate their key for bragging rights. However, they are unable to complete the Escape Room without the other groups so they inevitably offer support towards the end.

Many of my Escape Rooms last for about 40-50 minutes, however, when starting out, I would advise creating a small, 15-20-minute challenge which has about 3-4 tasks per group.

Due to the time and energy that can go into developing a lesson like this, it would be very disheartening for it all to come unstuck. The longer a room is and the more tasks it incorporates, the more chance there is for something to go wrong. If your first experience is an epic failure, it will be very difficult to get the confidence to give it another go.

1a) Put students into groups – I use ribbons to split the class into colour coordinated groups, the constant visual is beneficial for students and the coordinating teacher to manage the lesson. Obviously anything similar can be used for this purpose.

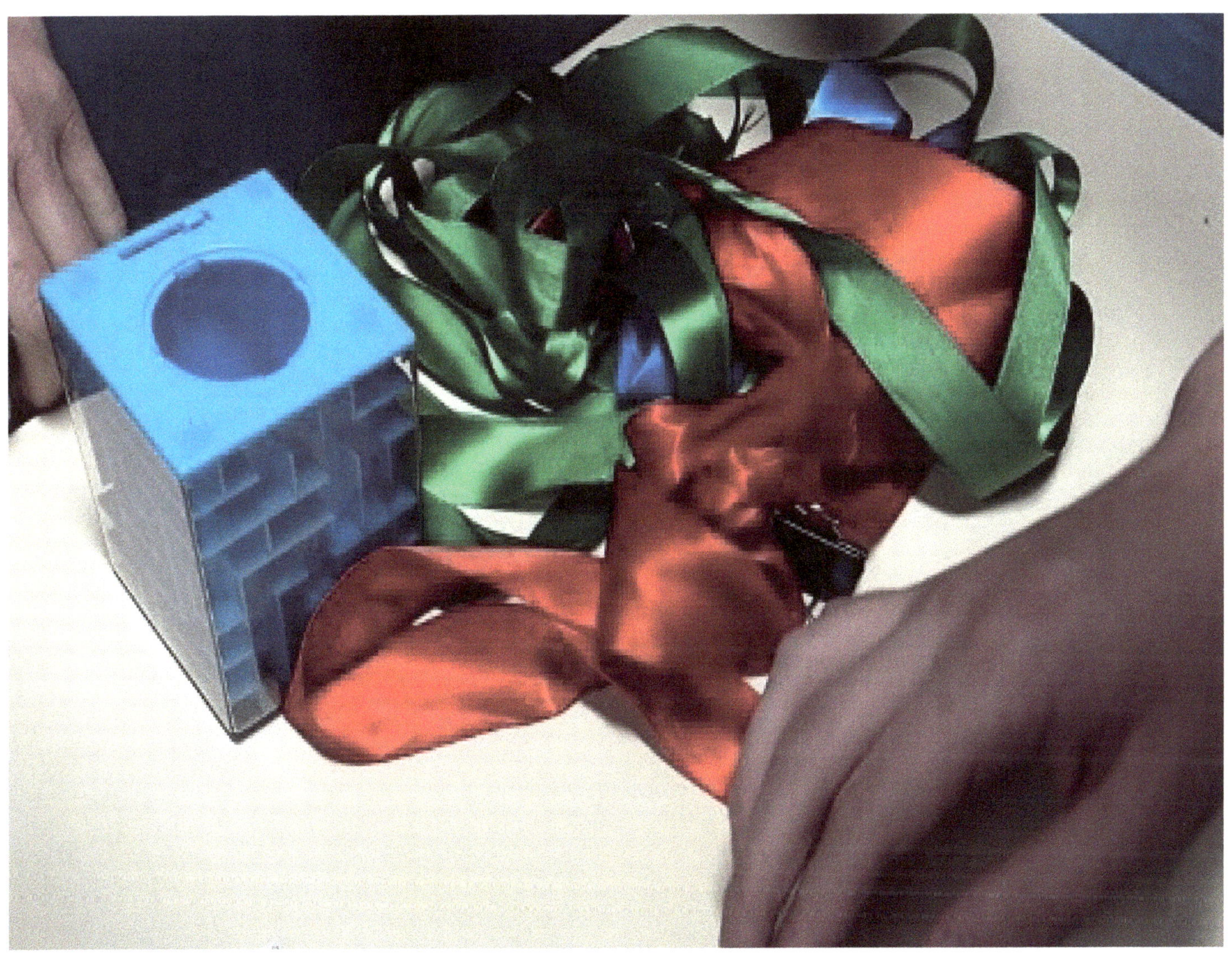

Coloured ribbons which the students wear to indicate which group they are in.

1b) Sort out groups prior to the lesson - The class below were mature enough to create their own groups prior to the lesson. This will be beneficial for a few reasons as it will create excitement through anticipation. Promoting the lesson well prior to the delivery is a perfect way of creating hype amongst the learners.

Students have selected their groups and are ready for the challenge

1c) Designate an area of the class for each group - This will help manage potential WHS concerns and also creates a strong sense of teamwork and comradery amongst peers.

Students have been given a designated area of the classroom to complete their challenges

<u>#2 – Accumulate Escape Room Resources</u>

The best resources you can gather are ones that can be reused across multiple different rooms.

Check out dollar stores, hardware stores, Amazon, E-Bay. Sometimes finding a cool Escape Room resource is enough to motivate you into designing a room.

<u>Resource table:</u>

Below is a list of resources that I have accumulated over the years which regularly make appearances in my personalised Escape Rooms.

Resource/s:	Description:	Additional information
3–4-digit number locks	Conceal a clue/task by using a 3-4 digit number lock.	Use a variety of numeracy challenges throughout your Escape Rooms. Ensure you get resettable ones so you can get more use out of them.
4-5 letter word locks	Conceal a clue/task by using a 4-5 letter word lock.	Typically, I will brainstorm a bunch of relevant 4-5 letter words that I can use these for (think key terms of your topic) Ensure you get resettable ones so you can get more use out of them.
Directional lock	These allow you to input multiple directions which will act as the solution.	Typically I will test out students mapping and cardinal directions with this lock.
Hasp Lock	These locks are awesome!! It allows you to conceal up to six different locks before allowing progression.	Typically, I use the hasp lock to conceal the final task. Each team needs to unlock their colour coded lock on the hasp lock but cannot progress until the other teams have finished.

Coloured key operated locks	Colour coded locks are great for identifying which teams need to crack which locks.	You can hide the keys in boxes, keep them on you, hide them in drawers, plenty of options.
Cypher wheels	Cypher wheels are always a handy Escape Room resource as they will allow students to decode a message which will be relevant to their next challenge. High quality, pre-made, content specific ones can be purchased, however, for those on a budget, they can be made easily for free using cardboard.	Get Shopping – Many awesome Escape Room props can be purchased online – These beauties were purchased on Amazon.
Invisible Ink pens and UV lights	These are an absolute must. If you are struggling for a way to connect challenges together, these allow you to tell students how to proceed to the next challenge. All you need to do is write a secret message on a piece of paper using an 'invisible ink pen' and get them to discover it with a UV light.	Using dark spaces and reveal zones make students feel like they are detectives.
Cryptex:	Cryptex: This can be reset to any 6 letter word. It also allows you to conceal a message inside of it. The best thing about this Escape Room prop is that it can be reset, therefore you can use it for multiple different challenges. All you need to do is figure	I have concealed things inside such as a USB, notes, puzzle pieces etc. A rather expensive resource, however, it can store resources, be reset to any 6 word term and is quite durable.

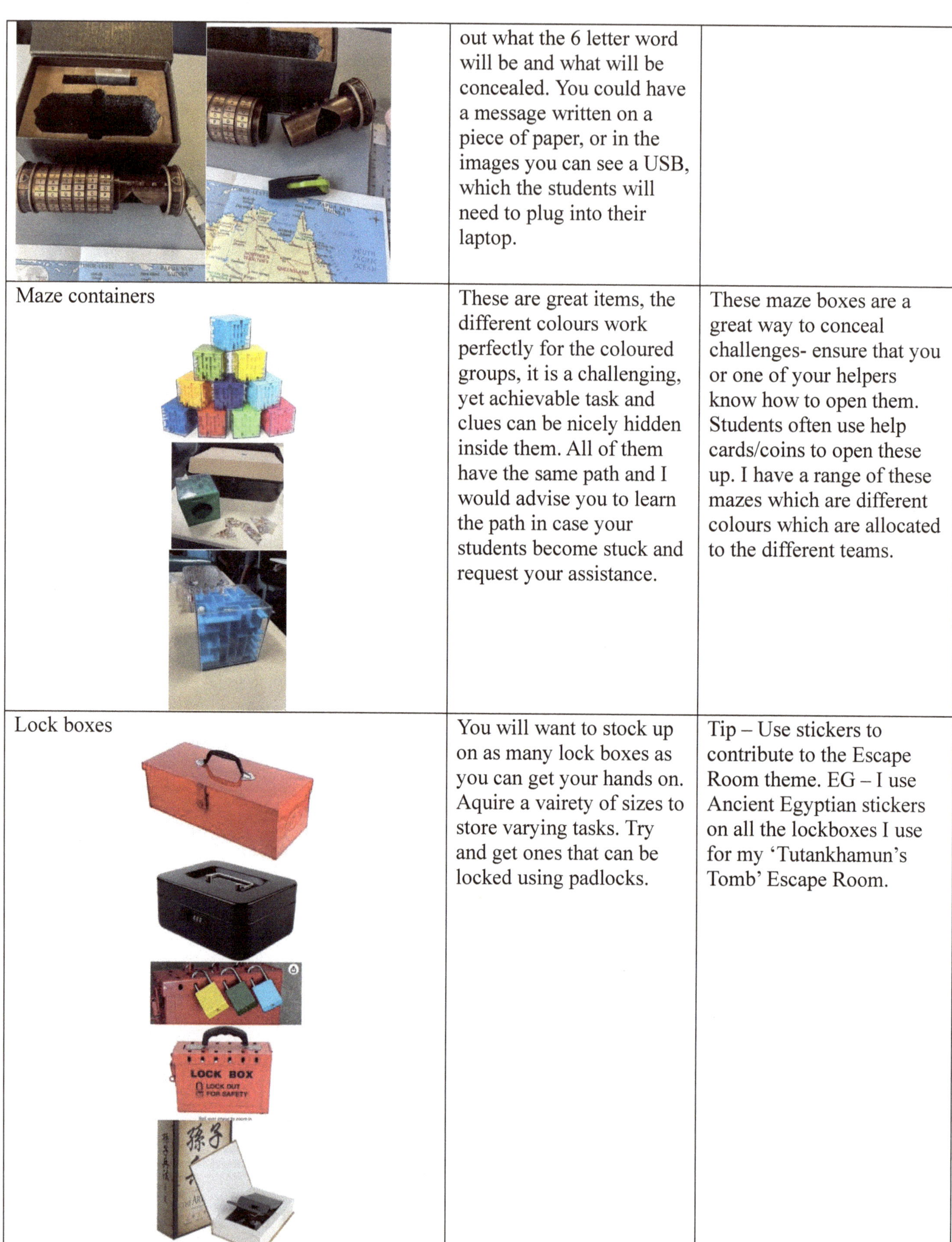	out what the 6 letter word will be and what will be concealed. You could have a message written on a piece of paper, or in the images you can see a USB, which the students will need to plug into their laptop.	
Maze containers	These are great items, the different colours work perfectly for the coloured groups, it is a challenging, yet achievable task and clues can be nicely hidden inside them. All of them have the same path and I would advise you to learn the path in case your students become stuck and request your assistance.	These maze boxes are a great way to conceal challenges- ensure that you or one of your helpers know how to open them. Students often use help cards/coins to open these up. I have a range of these mazes which are different colours which are allocated to the different teams.
Lock boxes	You will want to stock up on as many lock boxes as you can get your hands on. Aquire a vairety of sizes to store varying tasks. Try and get ones that can be locked using padlocks.	Tip – Use stickers to contribute to the Escape Room theme. EG – I use Ancient Egyptian stickers on all the lockboxes I use for my 'Tutankhamun's Tomb' Escape Room.

USB's	USB's are relatively cheap and allow you to incorporate digit tasks into your Escape Rooms. I will usually store a document on there and ensure a school laptop is available for the students to plug it into.	The tasks on the USB's can range from something as simple as a word document which, when opened, reveals an instruction for students to follow. It could also range to a more complex task, like a hyperlink which takes them to a website and requires them to do an internet-based challenge in order to proceed.
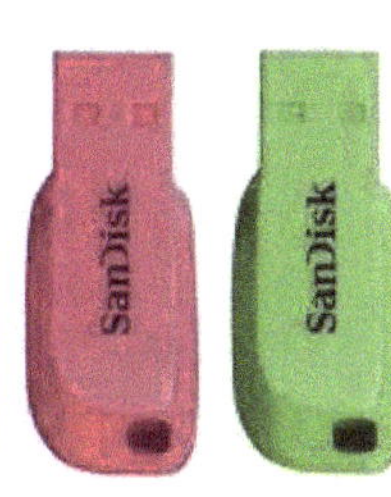 Magnetic locks 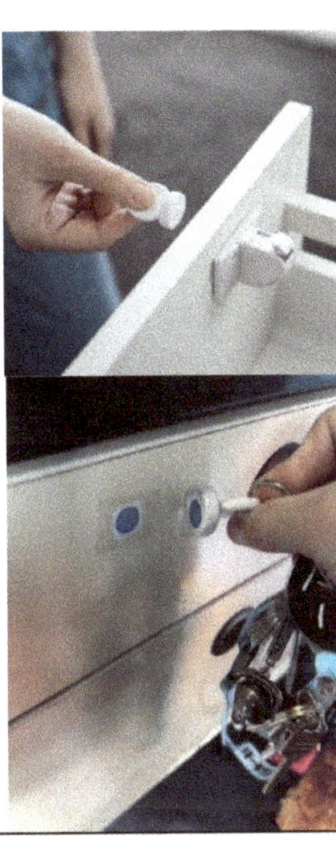	I repurposed my child proof magnet locks when my children got a bit older, now it is a great way to conceal tasks in some of the draws around the class. Perhaps you may have friends or family who no longer require them?	Magnetic child proof locks. Once you have tuned your brain to an Escape Room Design frequency you will be able to think of creative new ways to give life to redundant objects. My kids have grown out of the stage of opening all cupboard doors, so we removed the child proof locks. Normally I would have just thrown them away, now they are a regular object used for my Escape Rooms.
Resettable safes 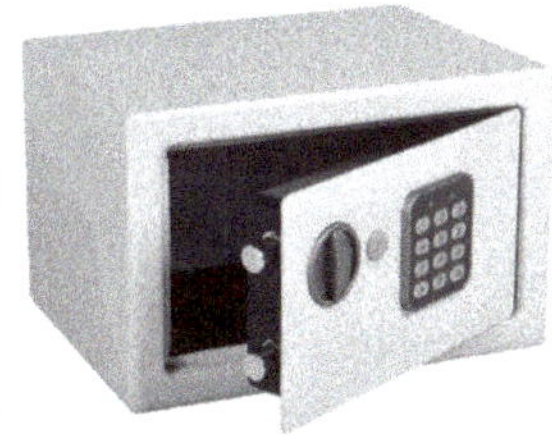  	Resettable safes like the one pictured are handy resources to have. It allows you to set a range of either number or letter codes. Sometimes the tricky thing can be actually opening it after putting in the correct code. For instance, this one requires you to press # and turn to the right, so I write that explicitly above the panel. (see images)	Although, rather expensive, they are heavy duty, reusable and a rather exciting object to open.

Breakout EDU kits 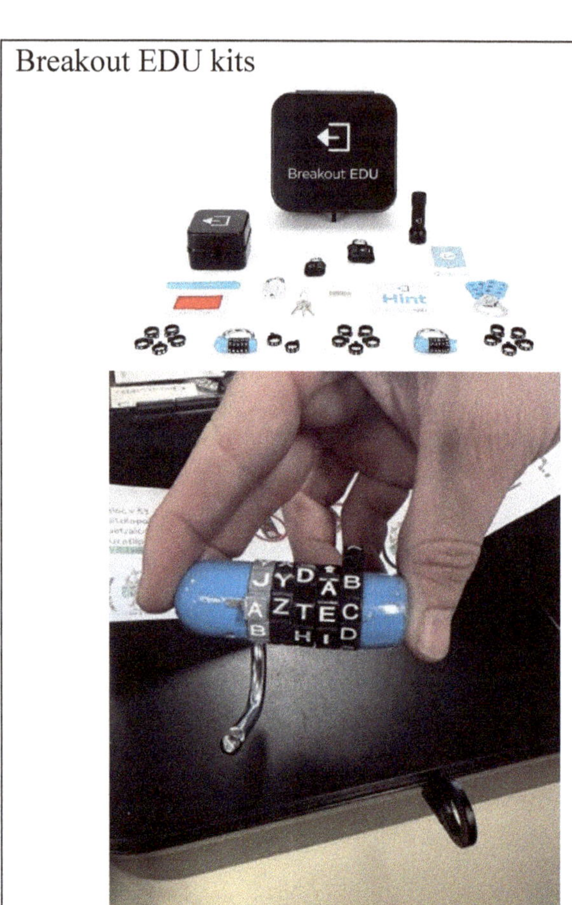	Our school has purchased 6 of these kits which have a fanatstic amount of resources to well and truly get you started. I have reached out to Breakout EDU and if you reference this book they will offer you free international shipping.	Knowing that the Breakout EDU boxes contain 5 letter locks which can be changed. When brainstorming ideas for challenges, I come up with various 5 letter words which are relevant to our topic which can be used.
Blank puzzles 	These are a great way for you to test out your artistic skills. Alternatively, you can print out images and add them to the blank puzzle.	It is an ideal opportunity to reinforce your theme by making the image relevant. Using secret messages which are revealed once the puzzle is completed is an effective way of incorporating this Escape Room resource.

Fake coins		I have found multiple uses of fake coins. They can be used as props, in numeracy challenges and as assistance tokens.	Assistance tokens are an absolute must. For anyone who has done an Escape Room challenge before you will understand the importance of having a way to assist students.
Stickers		These are a low-cost and effective way of allocating tasks to the different groups. For example, if you have a safe that needs to be opened by the red team, put some red stickers over it.	This is the easiest way to ensure that teams stick to their own challenges.
Torches		I will usually dim the lights and make it quite dark in my Escape Rooms. It creates an eerie environment and contributes to the immersion and suspense.	Glow in the dark torches and lanterns are perfect props to utilise. Turn the lights off or dim them and get the students to navigate the room using the lanterns. This will add to the immersive nature of the task while also reinforcing the colour-coded groups.
Ribbons		I use ribbons to split the class into groups, the constant visual is beneficial for students and the coordinating teacher to manage the lesson. Obviously, anything similar can be used for this purpose.	Hit your PDHPE/Sport department up, they always have a way of setting teams.

Captain Armbands	I would definitely advise that you allocate captaincy to one of the students. Sometimes disagreements can emerge when opinions and approaches differ. A simple appointment of a team captain usually alleviates most discrepancies.	An added bonus is that it enhances leadership capacity amongst students.
LEGO Model	If you don't mind spending a lot of money, this is an example of the sort of thing that can be purchased on Amazon.	I didn't actually buy it for an Escape Room prop, most of the things I have in my classroom are there purely for their aesthetic appeal, but once the Escape Room design frequency has been tuned in, anything and everything becomes a potential Escape Room prop.
Keyboard	Use old technology – Once you have tuned your brain to an Escape Room Design frequency you will be able to think of creative new ways to give life to old technology. My old phone and keyboard were sitting in my closet for years.	These are great props for revealing secret messages. With the keyboard, I took the keys out and rearranged them. Students then needed to find a standard keyboard in order to decipher the message.

<u>#3 – Get actively involved and dress up!</u>

It is common knowledge around my school that I will look for any opportunity to dress up. A major reason why I do this is because I want students to see that I am prepared to take risks and take myself out of my comfort zone.

Escape Rooms are a fantastic excuse to dress up and the benefits are multifaceted. It contributes significantly to the immersion of the Escape Room. I advertise in advance that I will be dressing up as a special character for the Escape Room and many students are eager to see what I have dressed up as. Furthermore, when students see that their teacher has gone to such extreme lengths to create an engaging learning experience for them, a stronger rapport is often developed. I also see dressing up and not taking myself too seriously, on occasion, to be a way of promoting resilience and strength of character in my classroom.

Year Group – Year 7

Topic – The Aztecs

Character – The Snake Lady

Escape Room Theme – The students are Aztecs and need to save Montezuma who has been imprisoned by Hernan Cortez.

Year Group – Year 7

Topic – Medieval Europe

Character – Knight (Sir Caryington)

Escape Room Theme – Students need to find the antidote to the Black Death

Year Group – Year 7

Topic – Ancient Greece

Character – Hermes

Escape Room Theme – Students need to find and return Zeus's thunderbolt.

Year Group – Year 7

Topic – Ancient China

Character – Buddha

Escape Room Theme – Students are trapped in Emperor Qin Shi Huangdi's tomb and need to find a way out.

Year Group – Year 7

Topic – Japan under the Shoguns

Character – Samurai/Tokugawa Kyarii

Escape Room Theme – The students are Samurai and Daimyo and need to work together to stop the invading Mongolians.

Year Group – Year 12

Topic – Sparta

Character – The Delphic Oracle

Escape Room Theme – Escape the Spartan Agoge (Their education system)

Year Group – Year 12

Topic – Pompeii and Herculaneum

Character – Bacchus/Dionysus (God of Wine)

Escape Room Theme – The students are roman citizens and need to escape the eruption of Mt Vesuvius.

Year Group – Year 12

Topic – Fall of the Roman Republic

Character – Cicero

Escape Room Theme – The students need to defeat Cato and Bibulus and save the republic.

Year Group – Year 11

Topic – The Trojan War

Character – Odysseus

Escape Room Theme – The students need to defeat deafeat the Trojans by completing challenges which helps them create a giant wooden horse.

Year Group – Year 11

Topic – Tutankhamun's Tomb

Character – Osiris

Escape Room Theme – The Students have entered the Ancient Egyptian afterlife. Osiris is testing them all to see if they have what it takes to progress to the field of peace.

Year Group – Year 12

Topic – Julius Caesar

Character – Adrian Goldsworthy (Post-Revisionist Historian)

Escape Room Theme – The students need to gather evidence of an assassination plot and present it to Julius Caesar before it is too late!!!

<u>#4 –Make it challenging, yet achievable.</u>

The aim of these Escape Rooms is to challenge, however, ultimately, it is better if the groups are able to achieve their objective. Therefore, I always have an element where the groups can seek assistance.

For those of you who have tried a commercial Escape Room out, you may understand how frustrating it can be to be stuck on a clue for a long period of time. I would strongly advise you to have a system in place where students can request assistance if they are stuck at any point. Below are some of the strategies I have used.

Assistance Cards – These can be handed in when explicit guidance is required. Students must use them wisely as they are only given 3.

Assistance Coins (denarii/sesterces) – Ancient Roman Escape Rooms - These can be handed in when explicit guidance is required. Students must use them wisely as they are only given 3.

Lady Fu Hao Coins – Shang Dynasty/Ancient China Escape Room - These can be handed in when explicit guidance is required. Students must use them wisely as they are only given 3.

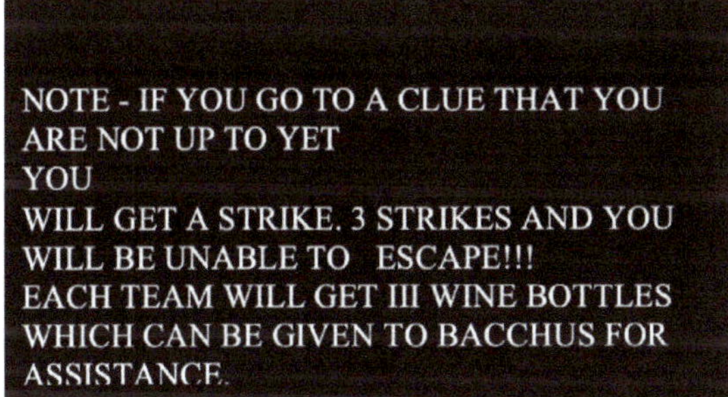

Wine Tokens – Get help from Bacchus

Completing the challenge requires a collaborative effort and as such should be celebrated as a class. Use whatever props are available and take a photo to document these experiences. A bonus is that these can come in handy for end of year reflections, graduations, newsletters and social media posts.

Victory Photos – Once achieved, it is absolutely vital that you take the opportunity to celebrate the collaborative effort of the class.

Year 12 2024 students celebrate their successful completion of the Julius Caesar Escape Room. These photos are excellent to use for yearly reflections, graduations, social media posts, newsletters etc.

Year 12 2024 students celebrate their successful completion of the Sparta Escape Room.

Year 12 2025 students celebrate their successful completion of the Pompeii and Herculaneum Escape Room.

Year 11 2025 students celebrate their successful progression through the Ancient Egyptian afterlife.

Year 7 2023 students celebrate their successful completion of the Ancient Greece Escape Room.

Year 7 2023 students celebrate their successful completion of the Aztec Escape Room.

Year 12 2023 students celebrate their successful completion of the Sparta Escape Room.

Year 12 2022 students celebrate their successful completion of the Roman Republic Escape Room.

Year 12 2024 students celebrate their successful completion of the Roman Republic Escape Room.

#5 – Get the family involved

From my experience, students love it when you build rapport with them by connecting with them on a personal level. One of the things I have done is put together video clues using my son and daughter.

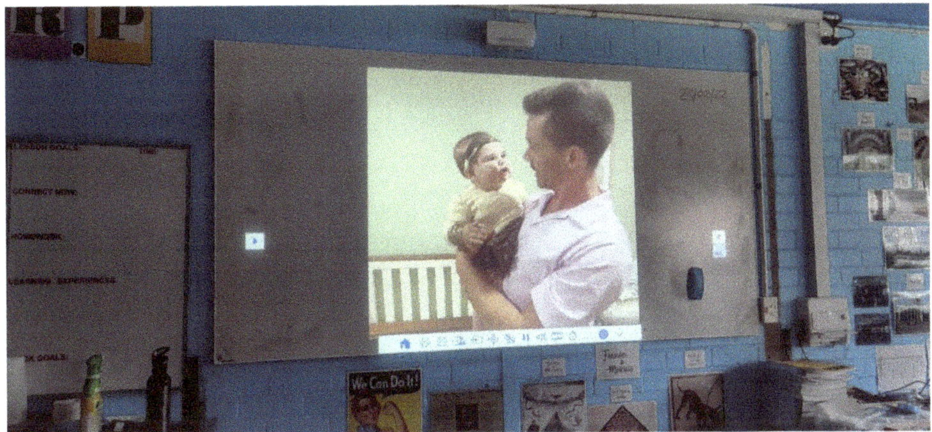

My baby boy Oliver featuring in an introduction to the Sparta Escape Room. He was deemed unfit for the Spartan state and was sent to the Taygetus mountains.

My daughter Eva featuring in a Spartan Escape Room challenge. She asked a question which would reveal a secret code.

Both children welcoming my students to the Tutankhamun's Tomb Escape Room.

<u>#6 – Venture beyond the classroom</u>

Despite this being labelled as an Escape Room, we aren't allowed to lock them in a classroom for obvious WHS reasons. The upside to this, is you don't have to limit yourself to the confines of the classroom. The task below required students to use a map of the school to find the next clue which was hidden in the school's Ag plot.

Year 12 students using a school map to find their next task which is hidden in an ancient tomb

- A school map usually comes in handy for this, ask your office admin staff for a digital copy of a school map, a google earth image can also be effectively used for this.
- The blue arrow indicates where I have hidden their next clue/challenge.

Decorate your classroom space: The more decorated the classroom space, the easier it is to incorporate the walls into your Escape Room. I use colour coded 'fold back clips' to conceal various tasks.

I am lucky enough to have my own space and I have turned it into an immersive History hub which comes in extremely handy when it comes to directing groups to specific areas of the room for their next task.

<u>#8 - Use Escape Rooms to tackle curriculum demands – e.g. Embed numeracy, integrate skills, Aboriginal Education.</u>

One of our syllabus demands in HSIE is to embed numeracy throughout the year. Challenges like this are a great way to do this. The props/images for the task should be relevant to the Escape Room topic/theme to contribute to the immersion.

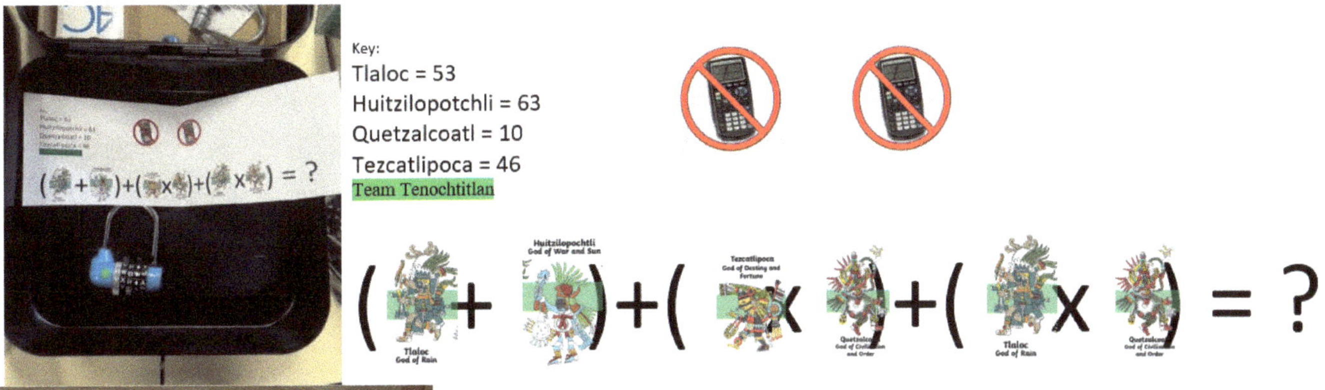

The images above demonstrate one of my favourite Escape Room tasks which involves both numeracy and content awareness. Students need to match the historical figure to the number to be able decipher the numeracy question. Then, without the use of a calculator, solve the question which will reveal a number code.

Students have become a little too reliant on technology which has resulted in some terrible numeracy skills. I like to take any opportunity to reinforce the importance of basic numeracy without the aid of technology.

Quite a few things going on in the images below – The groups had all found their key which opened the final clasp lock. Inside they found a key, a map and some poison (red cordial). They needed to get passed the guard by poisoning him which allowed them to open the cell to find Montezuma (which was the overall task).

Get senior students to help the younger classes. Great leadership opportunities. I have had success with disengaged senior students when they are given special tasks/roles.

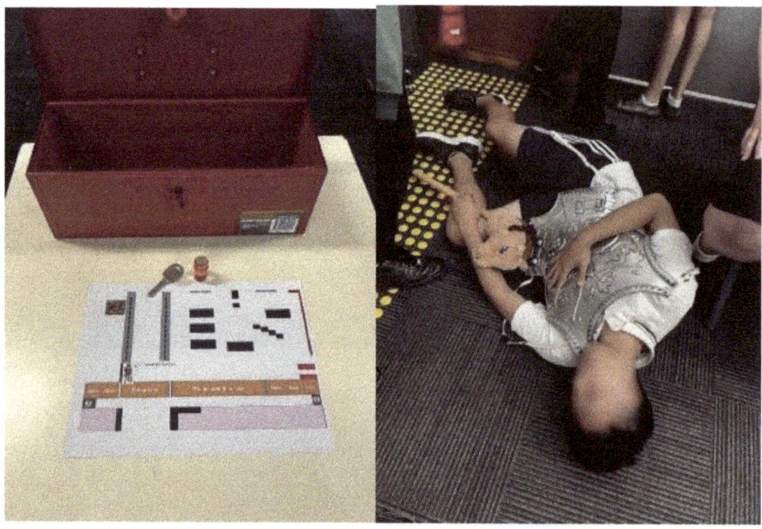

Students have just found a map of the library with a key and some bottled poison. When they make their way to the library a year 12 student is guarding a door. The map indicates that they need to give him the poison (red cordial). The year 12 student was prepped beforehand and ready to perform.

Cross class collaboration – Students in my year 11 Ancient History class studying 'The Shang Dynasty' created an Escape Room for my year 7 History class who were studying Ancient China.

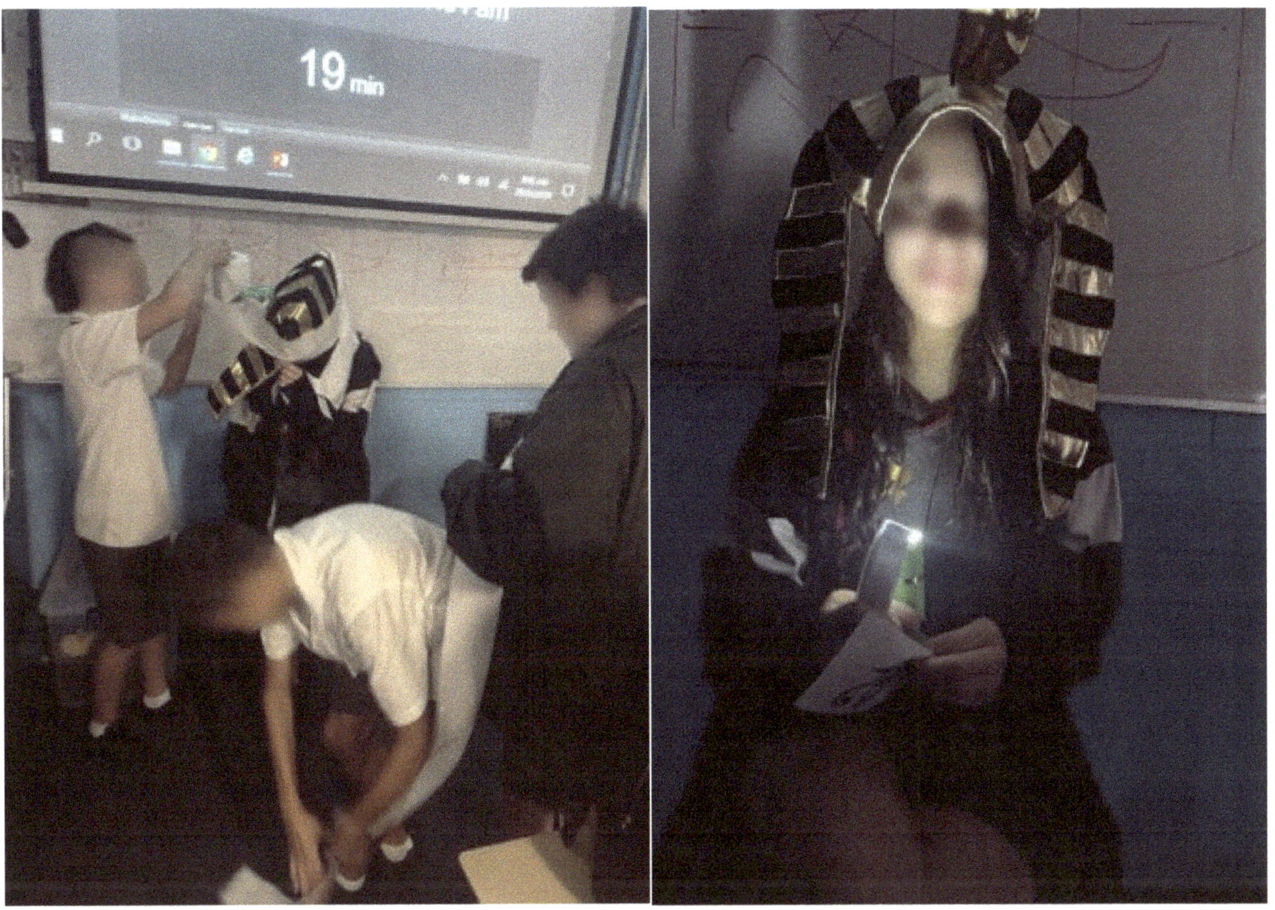

Cross class collaboration – Students in my year 11 Ancient History class studying 'Tutankhamun's Tomb' created an Escape Room for my year 7 History class who were studying 'Ancient Egypt'.

Ways older students can get involved:

- They can be a character
- They can run the Escape Room
- They can design the Escape Room
- They can be in charge of setting up/props
- They can be the photographer
- They can be a clue giver

Get students to help – Perhaps you could give a student a simple task to do. I was lucky enough to have significant overlap between my senior and junior class for one of my topics. So I allowed my senior students to design an Escape Room challenge for my junior students. The students came up with ideas I never would have thought of.

This is a tremendous leadership opportunity and fosters creativity and collaboration.

One of my colleagues being 'rescued' by students. She agreed to take on the role of Montezuma in our Aztec Escape Room. She hid in a room in the library until the students found the map with her location.

- Seek assistance from like-minded staff members.

Escape Rooms are not easy, however, they are worth it. There are so many ways that interested staff members can get involved. They can take photos, take on various roles, observe the challenge. Whenever doing an Escape Room challenge I will often send an 'Open Invitation' email, inviting anyone interested in observing into the classroom.

Bacchus and Isis were the teacher characters for this Year 12 'Pompeii and Herculaneum' Ancient History Escape Room

Another colleague agreed to take on the role of a 14th Century Pope to help the students overcome the Black Death.

Use your colleagues!!! Share the love. I have built an effective professional partnership with numerous staff members across the school over the past few years. These colleagues have been characters, secret keepers, assistants, observers, photographers. Their ongoing support has allowed the rooms to reach new heights.

<u>#11 – Create your own resources</u>

I have really enjoyed designing and making my own resources to use for my Escape Rooms. Despite being terrible at photoshopping images, it adds an amusing element to the lessons and the reactions from the students are always classic.

- Source Analyser – Once the overlay is placed over the top of the source, a 3-digit number is revealed which corresponds to a lock. A simple, cost effective, content specific challenge. And for some added flavour, Photoshop yourself in anything that you can. Most students get a laugh out of it.

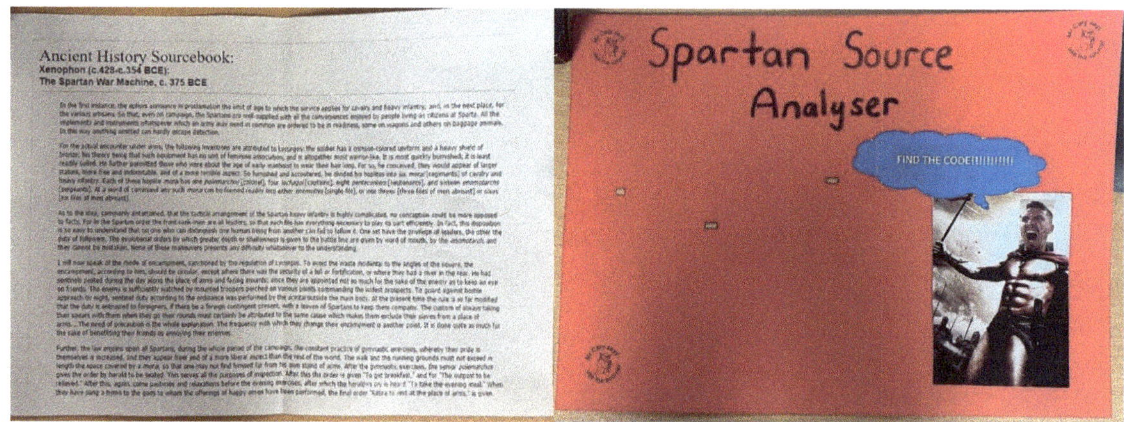

- Sewing needle tub- The tub is one of my personal favourite tasks. The idea came to me after doing an Escape Room in Campbelltown which had a similar challenge. It requires collaboration, out-of-the-box thinking, problem-solving and fine motor skills.

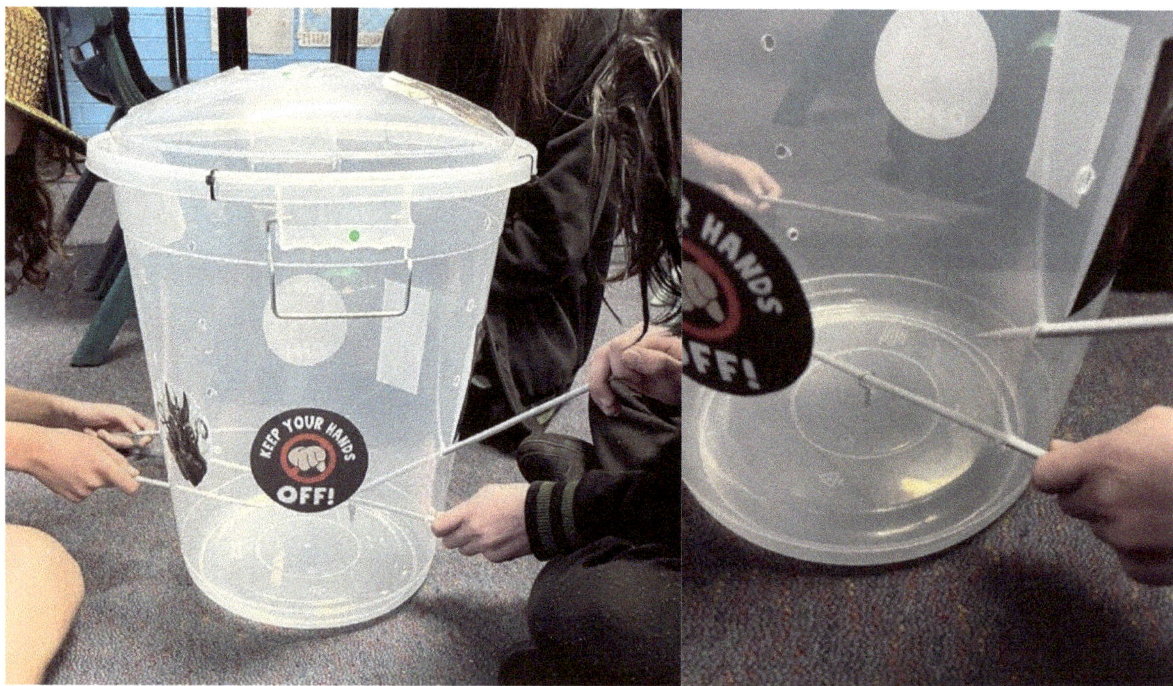

- DIY puzzles - You can purchase blank puzzles online at a relatively low cost. Once solved it could reveal a secret word, number, phrase or instruction. These could be written on the front, back or concealed in invisible ink. A cheaper alternative to this is to cut up a relevant image which students need to reassemble.

Year 8 Geography 'Water in the World' Escape Room – Solving the puzzle reveals instructions for the next task.

Year 7 History 'Shogunate Japan' Escape Room – Solving the puzzle reveals instructions for the next task. These instructions are concealed by using an invisible pen. Students must use the UV light to discover it.

Year 7 History 'Medieval Europe' Escape Room – Solving the puzzle reveals instructions for the next task. These instructions are concealed by using an invisible pen. Students must use the UV light to discover it.

Year 12 Ancient History 'Pompeii and Herculaneum' Escape Room – Solving the puzzle reveals instructions for the next task. These instructions are concealed by using an invisible pen. Students must use the UV light to discover it.

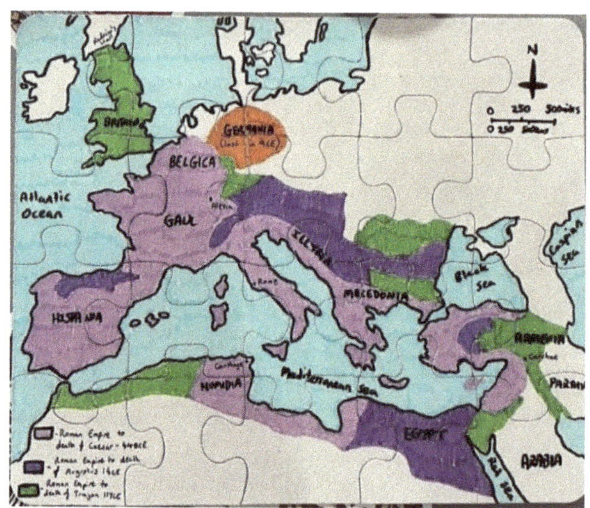

Year 12 Ancient History 'Fall of the Roman Republic' Escape Room – Solving the puzzle reveals a map, instructions have been given to them. Mapping/Geography skills are required to find the secret location which will open a 5 letter coded lock.

Year 11 Ancient History 'Troy' Escape Room – Students find pieces of the puzzle hidden throughout various tasks. The overall Escape Room mission is to assemble a wooden horse and present it to Odysseus.

- Colour lock

What is Medieval History also known as?
   a) The dark ages   b) The Middle Ages   c) The Viking Era

What years make up the Medieval period?
   a) 1500BCE – 500 BCE   b) 1500 – 2023   c) 500 - 1500

In what year did the Black Death arrive in Europe?
   a) 1348   b) 508   c) 1499

Which King Henry liked beheading his wives when they didn't give birth to a son?
   a) V (Henry the fifth)   b) VI (Henry the sixth)   c) VIII (Henry the eighth) 7 What nationality was Joan of Arc?
   a) French   b) Australian   c) Russian

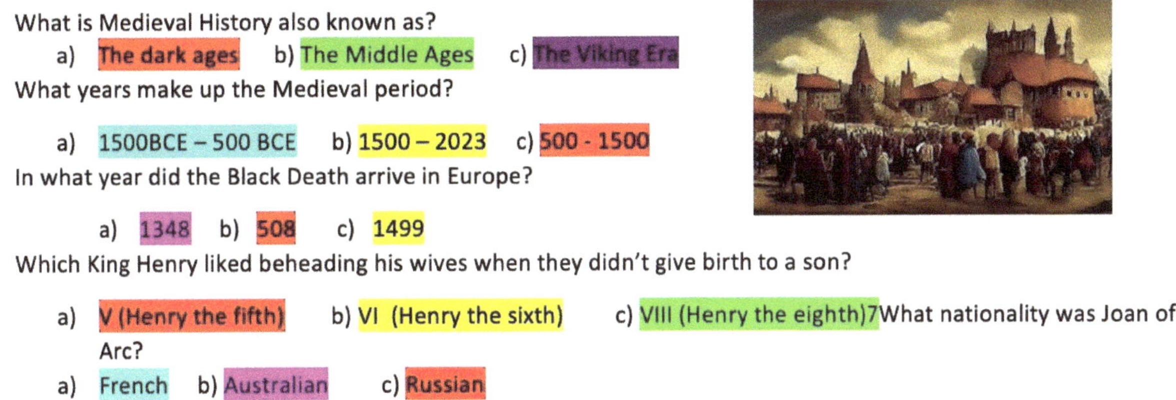

When students answer the questions correctly, a colour code is revealed. This will correspond to a BreadoutEDU colour coded lock

Breakout EDU colour coded lock

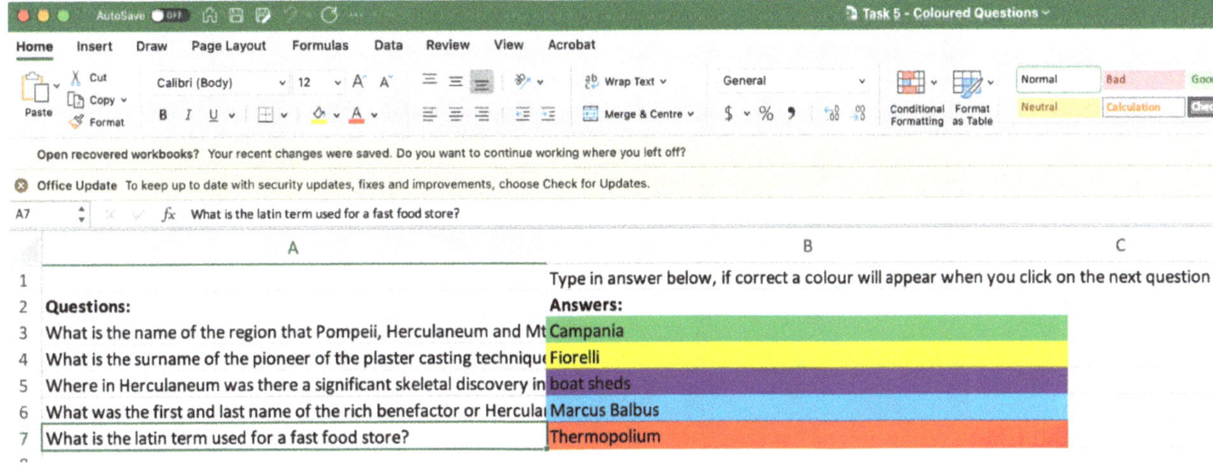

	A	B	C
1		Type in answer below, if correct a colour will appear when you click on the next question	
2	**Questions:**	**Answers:**	
3	What is the name of the region that Pompeii, Herculaneum and Mt	Campania	
4	What is the surname of the pioneer of the plaster casting technique	Fiorelli	
5	Where in Herculaneum was there a significant skeletal discovery in	boat sheds	
6	What was the first and last name of the rich benefactor or Hercula	Marcus Balbus	
7	What is the latin term used for a fast food store?	Thermopolium	

Microsoft excel has a function that reveals a colour when a correct response is identified. This excel sheet is put onto a USB and given to students when they open a lock box. My laptop is available for them to utilise throughout the Escape Room.

<u>#12 – Get Creative - Test out Escape Rooms yourself</u>

There is a wide-range of resources out there which will fill you full of ideas and inspiration. All you need to do is test it out. As you are testing any of this stuff out, ensure that you are actively asking yourself the question "what aspects of this idea can I take for my purpose?"

- Commercial Escape Rooms
- Boardgames
- Books

One of my guilty pleasures is challenging my friends with some of the Escape Rooms in Sydney. Whenever I attempt an Escape Room I am always actively looking out for inspiration for my own rooms.

Celebrating with my colleagues after yet another successful Escape Room experience in Sydney's CBD.

<u>#13 – Promote & Share the experience</u>

<u>Pre-heat the grill</u>

Lessons like this often require a significant amount of effort to set up. I will always let the students know about this. It is important that they know that these opportunities are privileges. In order to maximise the lesson for everyone involved, I would advise you to promote the experience. There are several ways in which you can do this:

- Get students excited about it. I will often tell students at the beginning of each term that there is an Escape Room challenge at the end of the unit. I will then proceed to tell them that the best chance the class has to complete the challenge is to actively engage in my lessons right up until the challenge.
- Prizes – offer prizes to students who excel throughout the task. Tell them prior to the task what prizes are up for grabs and what you will be looking for in your students. Lollies are the cheapest and most effective extrinsic motivators for teenagers.
- Make them guess what the Escape Room might be about.
- I will tell them that I will be playing a special character for the challenge and I tell them that I will be dressing up.
- Get them to choose their groups ahead of time, several lessons beforehand.

A collage of Escape Room images used to promote engagement on our social media platform.

Taking photos throughout the lesson will come in handy for multiple reasons:

- Share the experience with the community. These photos are often shared on our school social media account and community newsletters.
- Share the experience with a teaching network. I am a part of several History teacher networks and I will always share my lessons with them in the hope that it will provide inspiration to educators across the country.
- Put together a presentation for staff/teaching networks. If you are interested in connecting with staff members within your school and/or throughout the country. I thoroughly recommend volunteering to present 'engaging teaching and learning strategies' such as Escape Rooms in the classroom. I have presented at several staff meetings and conferences and the experience is always very inspiring and motivational. I have developed numerous professional relationships by doing this, which has resulted in the further development of engaging T & L strategies.
- Easy access to photos for graduation/end-of-year reviews. It is always a great idea to showcase your lessons at the end of the year to your classes to remind them just how much they have experienced and accomplished.

<u>#14 – Incorporate a mixture of challenges to appeal to a larger variety of students.</u>

Course content challenges:

Source Sheet: Primary or Secondary

Source Number:	Source:	Code Primary or Secondary (P or S?)
ꝺ	Thucydides	Circle the right one P or S
Β	A bronze statuette found near the Sanctuary of Artemis Orthia	Circle the right one P or S
Γ	Your favourite History Teacher	Circle the right one P or S
Δ	300 - DVD	Circle the right one P or S
Є	Video Game	Circle the right one P or S

Spartan Escape Room Task – Students must correctly identify the type of source that is pictured. Once this is done correctly a colour code will be revealed which corresponds to a Breakout EDU lock.

Breakout EDU colour coded lock

It is pivotal that the challenge continues to offer an immersive experience in relation to the subject/topic. Actively look for ways to link the challenges to the syllabus. The challenge pictured on the previous page requires students to analyse various historical sources in order to reveal a code.

Students using UV lights to discover secret words, numbers or phrases around the classroom, on objects or on paper.

- Content Specific Challenge – HSC key terms and definitions. When teaching senior students, it is always a delicate balance of trying to engage students and keeping the learning relevant. Escape Rooms can allow you to immerse students in key terms, people, events, and syllabus areas.

Students complete the maze which is concealing a content-based chronological order challenge. Once students correctly place the images in order, a phrase is revealed.

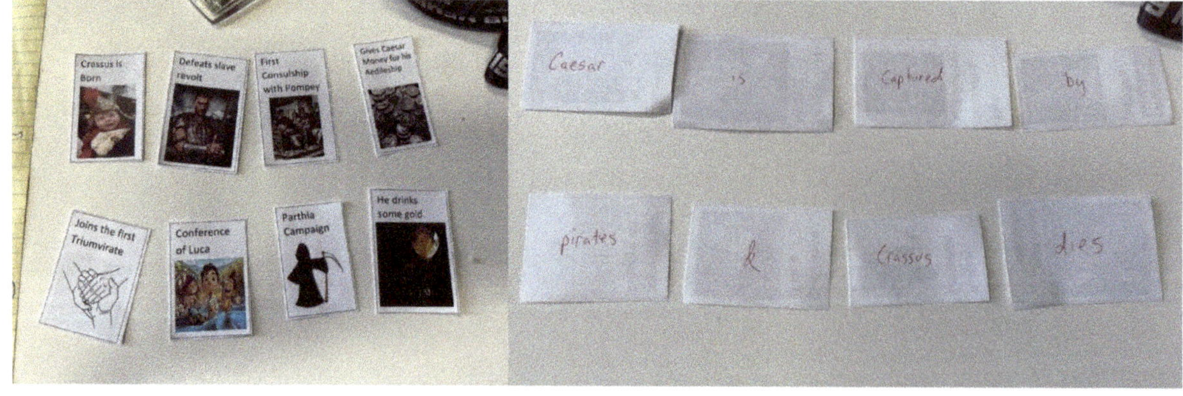

Students complete the maze which is concealing a content-based chronological order challenge. Once students correctly place the images in order, an instructional phrase is revealed.

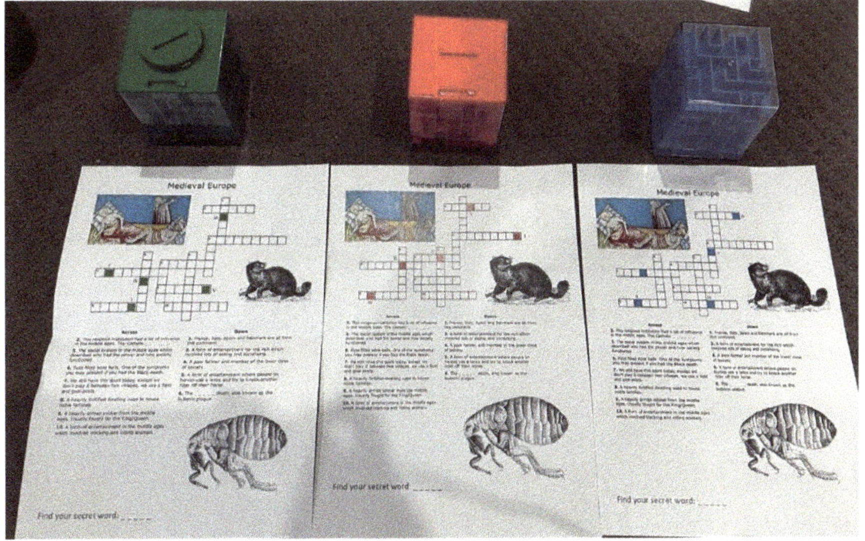

Students complete the maze which is concealing a content-based crossword. Once the questions have been correctly entered, the coloured squares reveal a secret word which corresponds with a Breakout EDU word lock

Due to there being a competitive element to the Escape Room groups, the best way to avoid students complaining is to design the same amount of challenges for each group that are of similar difficulty. As shown above, all groups complete the same crossword, however, the secret word has been changed using the coloured squares.

- Curriculum-based challenge – https://crosswordlabs.com/ - Numerous free online websites allow you to create your own crosswords. This challenge is used in most of my Escape Rooms. It is easy, cost-effective and a fabulous way of examining content.

The five spaces coloured in green are coded in roman numerals I-V. Once completed, a 5-letter code word will be revealed and will correspond to a Breakout EDU padlock which requires a 5-letter word to unlock.

🔥 Theme-based challenges

Try and make all activities related to your content/Escape Room theme. This will contribute to the immersive nature of the task.

- Find a words

Students find all of the relevant, content-based terms. The letters that remain, reveal a secret term which corresponds with a Breakout EDU lock.

Create your own find a word – There are numerous websites that allow you to do this, they are free and easy. https://thewordsearch.com/maker/

- Mazes

Students find the correct path using a highlighter. Seemingly, there are a bunch of random scrambled terms, however, once the path is solved, an instruction, question or code is revealed

Create your own maze – Sometimes one of the most difficult things to do is to figure out how to get students from one task to the next. The theme-based maze on the previous page can be used in a variety of different ways. Once the maze is solved, it can reveal a question, instruction, or code which can support the transition of tasks.

- Cypher Wheels

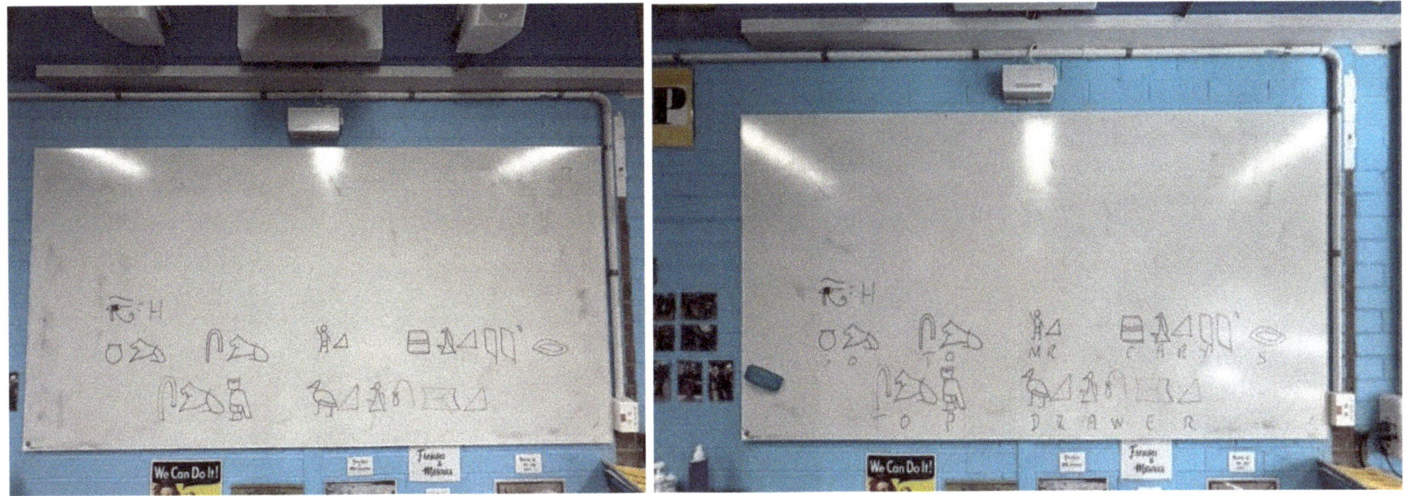

A cryptic message is displayed on the board when the students enter the classroom. It isn't until a group discovers the cypher wheel that it can be cracked. Once the code is cracked, an instruction is given to the students for the next task

Another example of a task that can be used to reveal a question, instruction, or code, are cypher wheels. These are a great way to support the transition of tasks.

🔥 Skills-based challenges

In the History classroom, we are expected to incorporate and examine historical skills throughout the year. Escape Rooms are a great way of embedding these core skills into the classroom.

HSIE skills that can be easily incorporated into an Escape Room.

- Chronological Order
- What Century?
- How long ago did an event occur?
- Map analysis

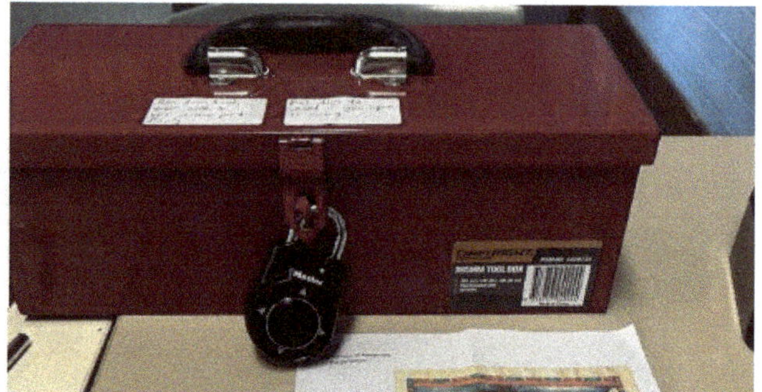

Lighthouse of Alexandria
to the pyramids

Nefertiti to King Tut

Mouth Opening to
Luxor

Chariot to the Sphinx

Heart weighing to
the eye of Horus

Cairo to Istanbul

Using the map provided, students are given a series of locations which reveals a combination of directions. These directions correspond to a directional lock which has been pre-set. This task was for the year 11 'Tutankhamun's Tomb Escape Room.

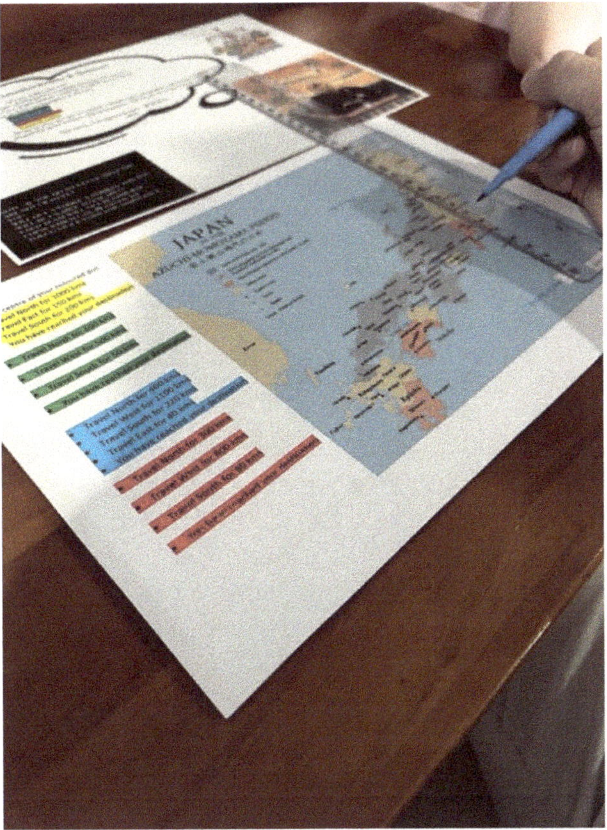

Using the map and ruler provided, students use the map key and a series of instructions to discover the secret city which corresponds to a Breakout EDU word lock. This task was for the year 7 'Shogunate Japan' Escape Room.

- Timelines and chronological order

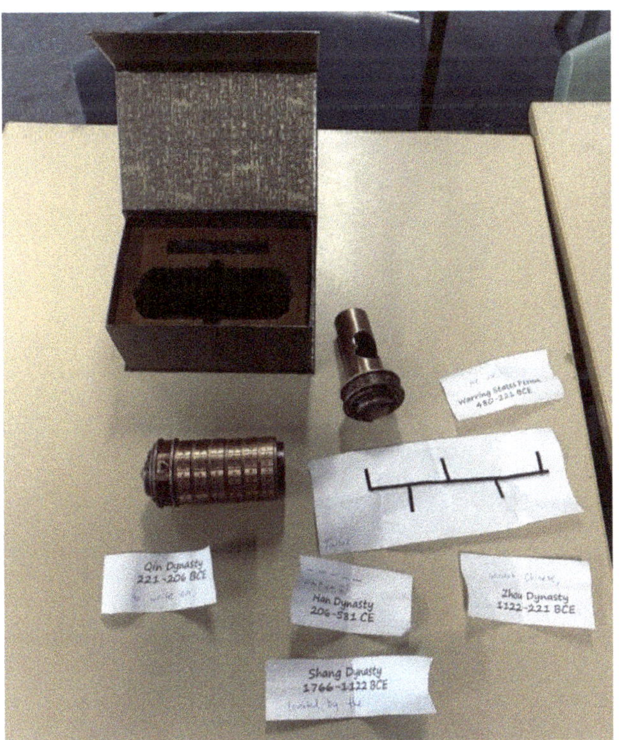

In order to reveal a question, instruction or code, students need to use their historical skill of putting key events into chronological order.

Alternative challenges

This is the part that has so much untapped potential when it comes to designing Escape Rooms. You can effectively test any skill.

Escape Rooms are a fabulous opportunity for a wide variety of students to showcase skills that they possess.

Students of all academic abilities can participate in an Escape Room challenge. Each student can bring a new perspective or a skill set which could greatly benefit their team. Whether it is quick mental math, an affinity for puzzles, or leadership skills, players can show off their strengths and feel good about their contributions. Success in an Escape Room really does rely on everyone bringing their own talents and skills and working together.

- Taste Challenge – Another immersive challenge which is easily adaptable. Because Escape Rooms are a strategy that I use semi-regularly, I try to ensure that my challenges have at least one 'new style' of challenge to keep things fresh and interesting.

If you intend on using multiple rooms throughout the year with the same class, you can always ask them for ideas on the sorts of challenges that they would like to see. Student voice is always an effective strategy, regardless of what you are doing.

'Pompeii and Herculaneum' Escape Room taste challenge. Using a visual key, a student is provided with a series of beverages. If the drinks have been successfully identified, a number combination is revealed which can be used to unlock the next task.

Song Challenge - Student groups need to sing in unison and key in order to progress to the next task.

Water Cycle Song

The Water Cycle 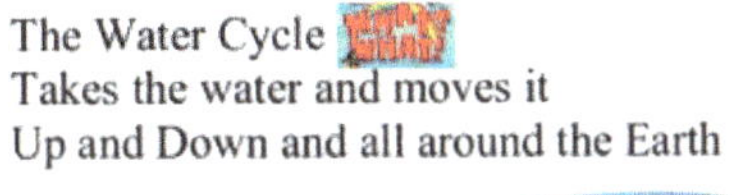
Takes the water and moves it
Up and Down and all around the Earth

Evaporation comes
When the heat from the Sun
Warms up all the groundwater
Then it turns to water vapor

Condensation takes over
It goes up to the clouds
Water vapor cools down
And it changes to a liquid, now

Precipitation happens
When the drops get big
It falls like Rain, Snow, Sleet, and Hail upon my head
I know it's the water cycle happening again
Evaporation, Condensation, Precipitation

The Water Cycle
Takes the water and moves it
Up and Down and all around the Earth

Singing Challenge: Mr Cary has your next challenge. In order to get it from him you need to sing the water cycle song together as a group. You need to do a good job with this and get it right. If the performance is not satisfactory, you will not receive your next task.

Year 8 Geography 'Water in the World' Escape Room Challenge. A group of students must sing the 'Water Cycle' song in unison and in key in order to progress to the next task.

Year 12 'Julius Caesar' Escape Room Challenge. A group of students must sing the 'First Triumvirate' song in unison and in key in order to progress to the next task.

- Physical challenge – these types of challenges are a perfect way of transitioning between tasks. You can effectively make students do anything to progress to their next task. Some of my Escape Rooms have required students to juggle, do push ups, do burpees, hold a plank, skip etc.

Year 12 'Sparta' Escape Room. Student group must complete 10 burpees in order to receive the next task.

<u>#15 - Create a fully immersive experience</u>

The best Escape Rooms that I have been a part of are the ones that create a fully immersive experience. With this in mind, I constantly strive towards full immersion with my rooms. As soon as I greet my students outside the classroom, they realise that the next hour is going to be awesome.

These are typically the questions I ask myself when developing my rooms.

- What relevant music can I have going on in the background to enhance the experience?
- What props can I use to scatter around the classroom?
- What character can I be and what can I dress up as?
- Can I get the students to dress up?
- Can I set the classroom up in a certain way?
- Can I put posters or visuals up on the walls?
- Can I act out an introductory scene or get special guests to do this?

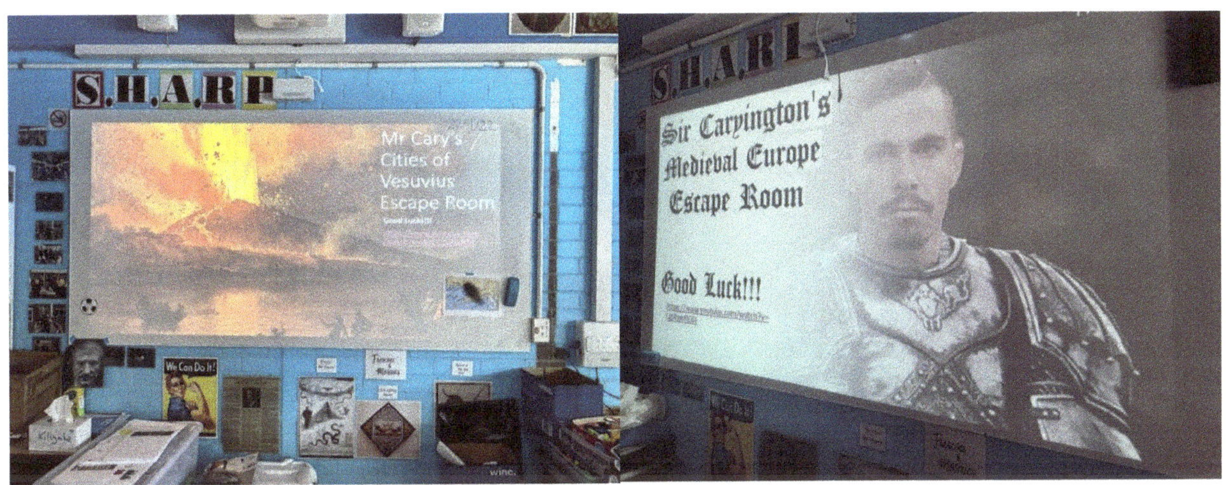

At the beginning of all Escape Rooms students enter the classroom and are confronted with theme appropriate music and visual stimulus to begin the immersive experience.

<u>What to do if things go wrong? Trouble shooting tips</u>

As I've incorporated over 50 Escape Room experiences into my classroom, I have compiled a list of potential issues that may present themselves with Escape Room implementation. I have also included some advice which will hopefully alleviate some of these potential issues.

- Issue: Students run out of time before they are finished. Advice: The first time you run an Escape Room, you don't have to have a time limit, just record the time that it takes them to escape/finish. It is ok to have groups that are unable to finish the task before the time is up; this is part of a challenge. My advice would be to reflect on it as a class and discuss strategies that can be done for next time to increase their chances of success. Sometimes students don't like things to be too easy. I would also advice on testing the Escape Room out on a small group of volunteers first to see if the room has been allocated an appropriate timing component which falls somewhere in between challenging, yet achievable.
- Issue: Conflict between group members. Advice: Conflict is natural when students are in a high-pressure environment such as this. I will often pre-emptively alert my student groups of this and tell them that in order to get more out of group members, encouraging the people around you is the best strategy. I will allocate the role of team captain to a group member who has the power to make decisions. You can offer

extra incentives to groups that demonstrate exceptional team work. An example of this would be to give out extra time on the clock or give them an extra clue token.

- Issue: Groups are stuck on a challenge. Advice: All of my Escape Rooms have a system in place to assist groups when they are stuck on something. A consistent system that works well for me is to use clue tokens/coins which all groups are given at the beginning. They are allowed to seek explicit assistance from me if they choose to redeem one. I will often carry around with me a clipboard with the solutions of the puzzles on them to assist in a timely manner during these moments.

The most important thing to comprehend is that you are not going to get it perfect straight away and that is ok!! Just like anything when it comes to educating our youth, our teaching and learning initiatives require constant reflecting and refining to reach proficiency. Hopefully with the advice in this book, you will experience less trials and tribulation.

Part 3 – A step-by-step guide to Escape Room creation

Designing your own Escape Room can be a fun and rewarding experience. Here's a step-by-step guide to help you create an engaging and challenging Escape Room:

Step 1: Brainstorm:

Get the ideas flowing, ask the following questions:

- What topic/unit of work do I want to design an Escape challenge on?
- What are some relevant terms I could use as 'secret words' – usually 4-5 letter words?
- What sorts of challenges could I incorporate into the room?
- How long do I want to give the students to complete the task?
- What will the theme be for the room? What do the students need to do in order to 'finish'?
- Which classroom am I going to use?
- When would I like to do this lesson? I usually make sure I have at least the lesson before and after off when doing an Escape Room.

I have found that once I have settled on a theme, it makes all the other steps a lot easier.

Step 2: Define Your Theme and Story

Choose a Theme: Decide on a theme for your Escape Room. It could be anything from a haunted house to a spy mission. The theme will guide the overall design and puzzles.

Create a Story: Develop a narrative that ties into your chosen theme. The story will give participants a sense of purpose and immersion. Consider incorporating a compelling backstory and a mission or goal for the players.

Step 3: Set a Difficulty Level

Know Your Audience: Consider the skill level of your target audience. Are you designing for beginners, enthusiasts, or a mixed group? Adjust the difficulty level accordingly.

Balance Challenges: Mix different types of puzzles (logical, physical, observation, etc.) to cater to various skills and interests.

Step 4: Design the Layout

Choose a Location: Decide where the Escape Room will be located. It could be a physical space or a virtual one.

Map out the Space: Sketch the layout of the room and plan where each puzzle will be placed. Consider the flow of the game and ensure there's enough space for participants to move around.

Step 5: Create Puzzles

Diversity of Puzzles: Include a variety of puzzles to keep participants engaged. Common puzzle types include riddles, ciphers, physical challenges, and pattern recognition.

Connect Puzzles to Story: Ensure that each puzzle is relevant to the theme and story. It should make logical sense within the context of the Escape Room.

<u>Step 6: Develop Clues and Hints</u>

Create a Clue System: Design a system for providing clues to participants when they get stuck. This could be through hints given by a game master, hidden clues, or puzzle-solving progression.

Gradual Difficulty: Make clues progressively harder, ensuring that players feel a sense of accomplishment as they solve each puzzle.

<u>Step 7: Build Props and Decorations</u>

DIY Props: Create or gather props that fit the theme. These can enhance the atmosphere and make the experience more immersive.

Attention to Detail: Pay attention to the details in the room. The more authentic and well-designed the props, the more immersed the players will feel.

<u>Step 8: Test the Escape Room</u>

It can become frazzling when things are not going the way you envisaged during an Escape Room. The best way to limit the potential of this happening is to test the Escape Room out prior to using it on a class.

Beta Testing: Have friends or a small group test the Escape Room to identify any flaws or areas for improvement.

Iterate and Refine: Use feedback to make necessary adjustments to the puzzles, clues, and overall flow of the Escape Room.

<u>Setting up template:</u>

On the next page is an example template of something I will fill in when planning an Escape Room. It is vital that you think about how each step flows into the next challenge.

	Resources Required:	Set up Required:
Plot/Opening Scene	<ul><li>Anubis Mask, King Tut Mask</li><li>Amulets (Ankh, Scarab Beetle, Eye of Horus)</li><li>Book of the Dead</li><li>Team captain arm band (In charge of amulets)</li><li>Crossword hidden inside book of the dead</li><li>Laptop</li><li>Projector with volume</li></ul>	Projector on with opening welcome video with a recording of myself and Eva. Opening Scene of Osiris explaining the first task Congratulations Message is hidden in a Breakout EDU box with 3 coloured padlocks and a clamped lock which requires all the padlocks to be opened to get through.
Step 1: Cryptex	<ul><li>Cryptex with USB inside</li><li>USB needs to find a word on it.</li><li>Crossword</li><li>Pen</li></ul>	Cryptex is set to ANUBIS USB placed inside Cryptex Laptop has an exposed USB port Find a word has been put on USB
Step 2: Complete Find a word	<ul><li>Find a word</li><li>Image of pyramids on the back wall</li><li>Hieroglyph sheet</li><li>Pen</li></ul>	Hint = This word should help you find out where to go on Mr Cary's Ancient Wall for the next step. Hieroglyph sheet hidden behind image of pyramids
Step 3: Use the Canopic Jars	<ul><li>Canopic Jars with jumbled message on them 'The Key Is Behind King Tut's Golden Death Mask'</li><li>Butterfly Clip</li></ul>	Key Hidden behind Image of King Tut's Death Mask Canopic Jars have jumbled message on them, they are sprawled out on a desk.
Step 4: Lock Box	<ul><li>Lock Box and Key</li><li>Coloured key inside lockbox</li></ul>	Hide another lock box key behind Anubis's stomach Ensure blue lock box has cut up image of ceremony with secret message written on it

	• Cut up Image of 'Weighing of the Heart Ceremony' • Invisible Ink Pen • UV Light • Anubis Statue • Map of Ancient Egypt with directional task	"Inspect Anubis's Core, that's the key to success right there" Put Directional map inside Black Lock box.
Step 5: Directional Lock	• Directional Lock and container • King Tut Cipher Wheel • Whiteboard and W/board marker	Write Hieroglyph code on the w/board, have this displayed on the board from the beginning. The symbol cracker should also be written on the board – Eye = H Hieroglyph code = "Go to Mr Cary's Top Drawer"
Step 6: Solve Blue Maze	• Blue Maze Cube • Gods and Goddesses code • Coloured Key • Safe	King Tut is locked inside the lock box. Image of the gods and goddesses should be stuck to a desk. Put coloured key and Gods and Goddesses mix and match code inside Blue Maze "In What Year Did Howard Carter Discover King Tut's Tomb?" Set safe combination to 1922
Step 7: Image code cracker	• Images of ceremonies and Legend • Container and 3 digit padlock	Put Ceremony images and Legend inside the safe. Answer will be 480 3-digit lock is set at 480 with a container Container has a clear maze and a lock inside
Step 8: Open All 3 coloured padlocks	• Breakout EDU container with padlocks and clap lock • Possibly put final congratulations message inside Tut's Tomb wooden box	

Part 4 – The Rest is History (History-based Escape Rooms) – My Top 5 Escape Rooms.

Scan the accompanying QR codes to be guided through the set up of these rooms.

<u>My Top 5 Escape Rooms.</u>

#5

Year Group – Year 7

Topic – Ancient China

Character – Buddha

Escape Room Theme – Students are trapped in Emperor Qin Shi Huangdi's tomb and need to find a way out.

Year Group – Year 7

Topic – Japan under the Shoguns

Character – Samurai/Tokugawa Kyarii

Escape Room Theme – The students are Samurai and Daimyo and need to work together to stop the invading Mongolians.

Year Group – Year 7

Topic – The Aztecs

Character – The Snake Lady

Escape Room Theme – The students are Aztecs and need save Montezuma who has been imprisoned by Hernan Cortez.

Year Group – Year 12

Topic – Pompeii and Herculaneum

Character – Bacchus/Dionysus (God of Wine)

Escape Room Theme – The students are roman citizens and need to escape the eruption of Mt Vesuvius.

Year Group – Year 12

Topic   Fall of the Roman Republic

Character – Cicero

Escape Room Theme – The students need to defeat Cato and Bibulus and save the republic.

The Ancient History class of 2023 and 2024 had the most exposure to my Escape Rooms, so I decided to conduct a small interview with a few students. Student voice is often sought when designing my lessons. One of the most valuable things that an educator can do is actively look for ways to seek out student voice; their insights are incredible.

Pictured (left to right) – Lana Abood, Shivaun Chand, Mr Cary, Carmen Behrouzi

Year 12 student Ahmed Al-Khamees and Mr Cary

Question: What Escape Rooms have you participated in?

Response:

Student A: Tutankhamun's Tomb, Sparta. The Roman Republic and The Shang Dynasty.

Question: What sort of challenges are you given in these Escape Rooms?

Response:

Student A: Team working challenges, so everyone has to solve their own puzzle as a team.

And no matter the difficulty, everyone's going to start working together. Yeah, I second that. It's very collaborative where you can't just take over by yourself. You need a couple heads. It kind of forces you to work together and I feel it's really good, especially with being in a senior class. Also, there's riddles and there's puzzles and there's this little one-cube ball thing and he makes me do it every time.

Question: How many of your teachers utilised Escape Rooms in your classrooms throughout your schooling?

Response:

Student B: Mr Cary used them in History and Miss Rouen sometimes used them in Maths, which was really helpful as it somehow made maths enjoyable.

In primary school, every year we would do a big math Escape Room and the winner got a Cadbury chocolate bunny thing. And it was like groups of 20, so I think the smaller groups are more fun.

Question: Have you enjoyed your experiences with Escape Rooms?

Response:

Student A: Yes, I actually have a lot. I got used to this class and developed more confidence.

I feel like I've grown a bit more confident around these people, even though they're just school friends. I feel like these Escape Rooms and these tasks improve a lot of like the relationship around the class. I feel like when I first got here, I wasn't really like that cooperative. Now I'm like super confident to speak to my peers.

Student B: It also helps building class relationships, friendships. I think the class camaraderie, it builds camaraderie. And I think the Escape Rooms themselves have made our friend groups stronger because we then can socialize through it. And I feel like it makes learning so much more fun rather than just coming into class and doing a pop quiz or something like that. I find that Escape Rooms are something to be excited about. Yeah, we plan it. I love Mr Cary's class. And it also makes me feel welcome. I feel like when I see someone dress up, I'm like damn, he loves the class, he loves the teaching and he doesn't want the worst for me, he wants the best for me. Especially when he's wearing no shoes and dressing up as a female Oracle in the cold winter.

Student C: Oh, I feel like it's so much more fun to engage, like in something rather than just like textbook work or reading off slides. And it's also something to be excited for. It makes me want to learn. It makes me want to go home and revise the content. I need to know all of this. I need to know everything.

Question: Do you think that the skills that are tested in Escape Rooms have the potential to help you later in life?

Response:

Student A: Yes, because they help you with problem solving. And also under pressure. If you're someone that has a lot of issues in life, as we said, with the helping hands, they usually jump in and solve that pretty quickly.

Student B: Yeah, I feel like with some certain tasks, you take a longer time to finish them and that can happen in life sometimes.

Student C: I second the problem solving thing. I feel like it's really good, especially when something goes wrong during an Escape Room and you can't afford to lose time. You just have to pick it up and you have to get back into it.

Question: Do you believe that Escape Rooms have contributed to an enhanced understanding of content areas? So specific to ancient history, when you engage in the Escape Room, do you think it enhances your understanding?

Response:

Student A: Yes, it also helps with revising. Even if people don't know some specific things in the content, everyone around helps you process the information. I feel like with Escape Rooms, it improves your memory. For example, in a test or an exam, if they can't remember anything, usually with the tests and with the problem-solving that comes out of the Escape Rooms, I feel like it really helps students memorise and get more confident with a lot of things.

Student B: And you actually remember it because of the little tasks that you do instead of just writing it down. Especially when you're trying to remember key dates and stuff. OK, you're like, yeah, when was this war battle?

Student C: I feel like we could say more about this, feel like it's more of a fun way to learn. Especially if you are someone who is struggling to process some information. I feel like, as Student A said, it's much more engaging. It helps students learn quicker, with the people around them as well.

Question: Would you encourage other teachers to try out Escape Rooms in their classrooms?

Response:

Student A: Yes, absolutely! There's so much, even if there's a lot of content, you can fit that all into a little, like many parcels that leads to one lock or anything like that. It's a good way to put that much content into one little thing. I feel like some students need a bit of a backup, like a break to rest their mind from all this heavy content that they get. I would be a band six maths student if my maths teacher used Escape Rooms to do algebra problems.

Student B: Bro, if my Biology teacher was doing Escape Rooms for Biology, I would be their top student. Yeah, I feel like other teachers should really start improving their teaching in a more fun way, especially because of how some topics are really serious.

Student C: Though it is hard because in ancient, it's easy to like, it's basically a bunch of stories and it's easy to follow like a narrative and learn to revise and follow the story or whatever. For example, if like English wanted to do it, for example, if we're doing 1984, imagine you are John Smith and you're in Big Brother and now you have to fight to save them. It maybe depends on the class, but I guess maths, bio, those might be hard to grasp. I guess more practical subjects. Yeah, more practical or maybe modern history would be good with it, but it depends on the subject because I don't think a lot of them, it depends.

Question: Is there anything else you would like to add?

Response:

Student A: Teachers have the ability to control the perception that a student has for a subject. I used to love Maths, but then I had a teacher who never put any time or energy into getting to know me. Upon reflection, I think this is the reason why I don't like Maths anymore. The content hasn't changed; the variable is the teacher. I used to think I hated History, but then I started doing Ancient History with Mr Cary and it has somehow become my favourite subject.

Student B: I feel like for Mr. Cary, with his Escape Rooms, he puts a lot of effort and he has some really fun and difficult tasks. I feel like he's just really supportive and I feel like what comes out of his mind, it makes all the students love his class and that should be portrayed to every single class. Because seeing him be so passionate about setting it up and getting to watch us take photos, coming around to each group, like, what are you guys up to? Egging us on.

And it's all like a healthy competition in the class. I don't know, the environment just becomes so much, you bond so much more as a class.

<u>Access to Free Resources!!</u>

I have developed numerous Google Drives for each of my Escape Rooms. If you would like access to any of them, please do not hesitate to contact me via email.

Chad.cary1@det.nsw.edu.au

Looking for a way to ***escape*** the monotony of your classroom?

Looking for a way to ***maximise student engagement***?

Looking for a ***dynamic*** and ***innovative*** way to promote high-school education?

This resource has you covered!!

This book will expose you to the unlimited potential of personalised Escape Rooms.

Whether you are a beginning teacher or seasoned veteran, this book will offer you valuable insight into the practical use of this invigorating, high energy, teaching and learning strategy.

This book offers you:

- A step-by-step guide to personalised Escape Room creation
- 15 expert tips on maximising the effectiveness of Escape Room integration
- Access to free resources to help you get started or help you evolve your ideas

Escape Rooms make learning enjoyable and memorable. Students may become more enthusiastic about education when it involves interactive and entertaining activities.

Integrating Escape Rooms into high school education provides a dynamic and innovative approach to learning, addressing various aspects of personal and academic education.

Students learn best when they are engaged! Escape Rooms provide an opportunity for students to play active roles in their classrooms.

As Dave Burgess emphasizes in his 'Teach Like a Pirate' mantra "It's ok to have fun in the classroom".[3] To Utilise Seth Godin's 'Purple Cow' analogy[4], immersive Escape Rooms have the ability to transform lessons into a 'purple cow' for students. A 'purple cow' is something that is remarkable, unbelievable and that stands out from the rest. It is something you will never forget. This style of lesson will stand out to students. They are unlike the majority of teaching and learning strategies that they are exposed to on a day-to-day basis and thus will have a more substantial impact on their education.

---

[3] Burgess, D. (2012). *Teach like a pirate : Increase student engagement, boost your creativity, and transform your life as an educator.* San Diego, California: Dave Burgess Consulting, Inc.

[4] Godin, S 2009, *Purple cow : transform your business by being remarkable*, Portfolio, New York.

www.ingramcontent.com/pod-product-compliance
Lightning Source LLC
Chambersburg PA
CBHW042050010826
48978CB00023B/1355